Chapter 1

The playground at St. Felix's was a happy place to be, and the happiest kitten in it was Ginger.

He could climb the highest trees...and walk to the end of the flimsiest branches.

In class he was always the first to put his hand up when the teacher asked a question.

(Although he didn't always get the answer right!)

He could jump higher...

and further...

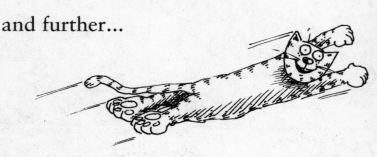

and run faster than
any other kitten.

If ever there was an emergency
in the playground, he would
undo his collar,
tie it round his
head and
leap into
action.

He became the highest scorer in the pawball team and was made captain.

Everyone loved Ginger and wanted to be his friend...

Everyone, that is, but the school bully, Tiddles, and his two henchmen, the Wilson Twins.

Tiddles hated Ginger. It was Ginger's fault that he no longer ruled the playground and that his gang was no more. He and the Wilsons lurked in the shadows waiting for Ginger to make a mistake.

He's so nice it makes me sick... He's such a goody two shoes... I'll get that Ginger for showing me up in front of the whole school.

If anyone came near, they would smile their sickly smiles.

RAAAR!

If it was just a little kit, they would sneer and snarl to frighten it away.

Chapter 2

But, Ginger was starting to get a little above himself.

In fact, he was becoming a bit of a pain.

One or two kittens were getting a bit fed up with him.

One day, as Tiddles watched
from the shadows, he realised
something very important.

After pawball practice Tiddles
crept into the changing room

While the team
were in the Groom
room, he quietly
lifted Ginger's
collar off its hook.

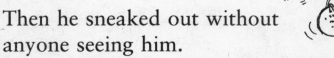

Then he sneaked out without
anyone seeing him.

I've got it!

Tiddles looked at it carefully. It seemed perfectly normal, in fact it was nearly the same as the one Tiddles was wearing. It had a metal tag on it with Ginger's name and address, in case he got lost.

When Ginger had finished licking himself clean he went to get his collar off the peg – but it had gone.

He searched everywhere. He looked in, on, under and behind.

He tried to remember where he'd been.

After a while Miss Tiffany came by. He explained his problem and they looked together but neither of them could find the collar.

She found him a spare collar in the lost property box.

In class, Miss Tiffany made an announcement.

No one appeared to know anything about it.

When he got home his mother was very surprised to see him wearing a strange new collar.

Can't you look after anything? I suppose some other kitten has got a nice new collar now. It may not have been very expensive but I went to a lot of trouble to find that one.

Yes, Mum

Mum fished around at the back of the airing cupboard and found an old collar that Ginger hadn't worn for a while.

Erk! It's too tight.

That night Ginger lay in bed
thinking.

Chapter 3

The next day Ginger's collar felt uncomfortable.

At breaktime the kittens played pawball.

As Ginger ran for an easy catch, he tripped and hurt himself.

He saw that Tiddles was watching and lost his concentration. He dropped catch after catch.

Ginger thought a really big throw
would impress his friends, but the
ball got stuck at the top of a tree.

Ginger climbed and climbed until
his head poked out at the very
top. He stretched and leaned
until he got a claw to the ball and
sent it falling down to the crowd
below.

Well done
Ginger,
you can come
down now.

But Ginger was stuck! He couldn't believe it. He was the best tree climber in the school and he was stuck! The more he wriggled, the stickier it got. It was so embarrassing.

The bell rang and the crowd below got smaller as the kittens drifted off to class. They said some nasty things about Ginger.

It took Ginger twenty minutes to climb down that tree.

He choked back the tears as he told Miss Tiffany what had happened.

Ginger Pickles! That's the most pathetic excuse I've heard all term and this is the second time you've been late for my class. What's the matter with you? Go to your desk right now and never be late for my class again.

Yes, Miss Tiffany. Sorry, Miss Tiffany.

Miss Tiffany was his favourite teacher. Ginger hated being in her bad books.

As he sat down, Ginger wished that the floor would open up and swallow him.

Tiddles sat
behind and
smiled. Ginger
didn't scare
him any more.

Suddenly Ginger had three
shadows. Tiddles and the Wilsons
followed him everywhere and
copied everything he did.

After a couple of days Ginger
could take no more. He shouted
at them.

When Tiddles tweaked his
whiskers, Ginger lost all control.

His eyes filled with tears – and he
lashed out at Tiddles. Straight
away he knew it was a mistake.

The Wilsons pinned his arms
behind his back and held him.

Tiddles marched up and down
the crowd of kittens that had
gathered to watch.

It was awful.

Tiddles and the Wilsons walked
away laughing. They left Ginger,
just a small, sobbing heap of fur
in the middle of the playground.

Chapter 4

The whole school had watched
but not one kitten came to help
Ginger. They knew he wasn't the
Ginger Ninja any more so he
couldn't protect them from
Tiddles. They were scared so
they made up excuses.

In no time at all, Tiddles had the playground under his control. His old gang were eager to join up.

Headquarters were set up behind the bike sheds and the kittens queued up, with their snack boxes, to pay their "taxes" to Tiddles.

Tiddles liked it best when it was Ginger's turn. Ginger's mum really did make the best fishybix. They tasted *so* good.

Tiddles used both his brain cells
to find other ways to upset
Ginger. He stuck a note on
Ginger's back, and, as everyone
was too scared to tell Ginger, he
wore it all day until it fell off.

He made Ginger say all sorts of
horrid things.

In class he found it hard to pay
attention and couldn't answer
any questions at all.

But soon it was only Tiddles that laughed at Ginger. Some of his gang felt uncomfortable. They thought that Ginger had learned his lesson.

Chapter 5

At the weekend, Ginger went round to see his grandpa. They were great friends and did lots of things together. Grandpa noticed that Ginger was not his normal, happy self.

Grandpa fixed Ginger with a stern look and waited until he'd finished.

What does your collar have to do with it? It's just an ordinary collar, isn't it? The strength that you've lost came from inside you. It's still there, and you still are the Ginger Ninja. You just have to believe in yourself.

Oh yeah, I...I... suppose I've been a bit silly haven't I Grandpa?

I think, maybe, you got a bit big-headed?

Well...y-e-e-e-s, maybe.

*Spread toast with garlic butter and chocolate chips then put cheese on top and grill until the cheese melts. It's delicious if you're a Ginger Ninja, (ask an adult for help!)

They sat down to eat. Ginger was so busy telling Grandpa what Tiddles had been up to, that he forgot that the cheesy dreams were hot.

Ginger had to drink three bowls of water!

I think there's a lesson to be learned here. If the cheese is hot in the middle, then you should eat the cool bits around the edge. The cool bits are like your old friends. Show them that you are a changed kitten and they will be your friends again. They will help you to get to the hot part in the middle.

Oh right! Brilliant! Tiddles is the hot part. Thanks, Grandad.

Chapter 6

Muncher Matthews wasn't called
Muncher for nothing. He was
always hungry. Ginger offered
him a fishybik.

To his horror... Muncher
realised...

...that he had eaten one of the
fishybix that Ginger normally
gave to Tiddles.

Tiddles was far too important to bother with the little kits, so he had put Muncher in charge of them. He called his little squad together.

Soon, everyone expected that
Ginger would do something
about Tiddles.

One by one the kittens came to
talk to him in secret.

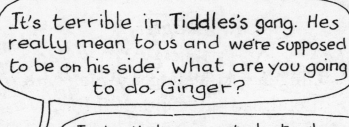

It's terrible in **Tiddles's** gang. Hes really mean to us and we're supposed to be on his side. What are you going to do, Ginger?

I don't know yet, but when I make my move I don't want you to do anything, understand? It's between me and Tiddles, ok?

OK.

But how could he get the Wilson twins on his side? He couldn't take them and Tiddles on together. They'd flatten him!

Chapter 7

Ginger was feeling happier with life already. He climbed the highest tree that he could find and whooped to the birds when he reached the top.

I am the Ginger Ninja!

He took an interest in class again
and, one morning, just before
breaktime, Miss Tiffany asked a
question that he could get right.
He stood up to give his answer.

It made him feel all warm inside
to be back in Miss Tiffany's good
books.

He was just about to sit down
when a tiny glint of sunlight
caught his eye. It was a reflection
from the clock on the wall. There
was something hidden on top of
it. If the sun wasn't shining at that
very moment, you would never
notice anything was there.

His heart skipped a beat.
Could it be? But how?
He must be mistaken?

The bell rang for break and the kittens filed out of the classroom. When Ginger was sure they had all gone he started to climb the wall.

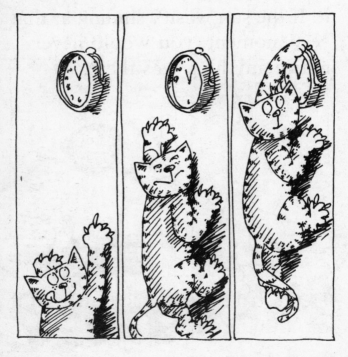

There wasn't much to get hold of and one of his claws split as he pulled himself up to the clock.

There, laid over the top of
the clock, was his collar! He
grabbed it and lost his foothold.

He fell through the air, but
managed to twist round and
landed gracefully on all fours.

He dusted his old collar and put it
on. Instantly he felt better.

Ginger strolled over to the bike
shed for the last time. He stared
hard at Tiddles and slowly
dropped fishybix in front of him.

Tiddles saw Ginger's collar and gasped.

Ginger smiled
knowingly and
walked away.

Tiddles stared at the Wilsons. The Wilsons stared back.

Soon they were bickering and, just as Ginger hoped, the argument turned into a fight.

Chapter 8

All the kittens were excited. By
the time the lunch bell rang, you
could almost taste the excitement
in the air.

Ginger had picked off the cool
edges of Tiddles gang. Now only
Tiddles was left.

He made his move.

But Tiddles's gang were nowhere to be seen.

Tiddles turned to the Wilsons.

Tiddles was starting to wish that he'd been nicer to the Wilsons.

Calmly, Ginger took off his collar and gave it to Tiddles.

He grabbed it and looked puzzled. He knew that Ginger was nothing without his collar.

Ginger leaned over so close
that his nose pressed against
Tiddles's nose.

Tiddles was almost hypnotised. He could see deep into Ginger's eyes. Ginger was so sure of himself that Tiddles couldn't be certain of winning a fight, even though he was bigger.

Help!

He turned away, throwing
Ginger's collar on
the ground.

Then he
spat and
sloped off
to kick the
wall behind
the bike shed
and curse the
day he ever
heard of the
Ginger Ninja.

The kittens swarmed round Ginger, pleased to be friends with him again, thrilled that the mean old bully had been seen off.

Ginger had learned his lesson the hard way and tried not to be big headed, but inside he was bursting with pride.